ne

A PICK-YOUR-PATH
ADVENTURE

WARNING!
THIS IS NOT
A BOOK

Moon Unit
A Pick Your Path Adventure
by Dan Metcalf
Illustrated by Maurizio Campidelli

Published by Ransom Publishing Ltd.
Unit 7, Brocklands Farm, West Meon, Hampshire
GU32 1JN, UK
www.ransom.co.uk

ISBN   978 178591 794 3
First published in 2019

MOON UNIT

DAN METCALF

ILLUSTRATED BY
MAURIZIO CAMPIDELLI

RanS:m

AUTHOR'S NOTE

If, like me, you love games and adventure, then you're in for a real treat.

Game books like this one are what made me fall in love with reading.

In fact, this isn't really a book at all; it's a fully interactive adventure that will have you guessing and guessing.

What happens next? You decide!

HOW IT WORKS

Start off with the introduction. That gives you two options. You can either pick an option OR you can just be random and flip a coin!

Go to the option you want, then carry on reading!

If you choose to flip a coin …

this is HEADS

and this is TAILS.

INTRODUCTION

As Chief Mechanic at Lunar Mining Unit One you've had 18 loooong months of mind-numbingly menial work. Now your day is about to get a little more lively ...

'Incoming ship!' cries your crewmate, Sammy. Outside, a strange-looking spacecraft with ultrablue thruster engines lands close to your mining rig. The comms screen hisses and buzzes, so you give it a good whack with your fist.

A disgusting, reptilian, alien face appears on the screen. 'This is the Krelurian Battlecraft Nomu. We have invaded your moon. Surrender or die!'

You look around for whoever is in charge, before you realise that it's you. So what do you do?

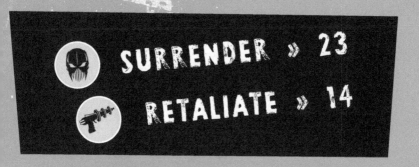

SURRENDER » 23

RETALIATE » 14

'We'll take our chances, thanks,' you tell the Grey. The grey alien appears to shrug (does it even have shoulders?) and the screen goes blank again.

'Back to square one,' sighs crewman Sammy.

'Don't give up yet,' you say, leaping up with a sudden burst of adrenaline.

There is a hum in the air and the Krelurian materialises in front of you.

Time for another decision.

RUN! » 17

ARM YOURSELF » 25

2

Missiles, huh?

You are found in the cargo bay and marched back to the bridge. The Krelurian general sneers at you.

'You dare to fight our mighty race? Who do you think you are?'

Smirking, you raise a detonator.

'Smarter than you, for one thing.'

You click the button and each one of those thousand tonnes of missiles speeds away, destroying the entire alien fleet.

SMART AND STYLISH!
TRY AGAIN?

You sit tight and wait. Soon a guard escorts you to the bridge.

'You have shown courage,' says the general, through his hissing, snake-like mouth. He seems to glow with pride. 'As a reward, we invite you to become an honourary Krelurian.' He holds out a medal and a handgun.

You are dumbfounded.

You look at them and don't move, mulling over your options.

ACCEPT » 13

DECLINE » 20

4

You drop the axe, defeated and ashamed. You bow your head.

'Wise choice,' says the alien. It pushes your chin up with its hands and looks you in the eye. 'You show spirit. You shall be my personal slave.'

'Thank you,' you mutter, hating yourself for saying it. 'Now what?' you ask.

'Now I infect your blood with microspores to show that you belong to me.'

He produces a syringe with a needle the size of your arm. Just the sight of it makes you wince. 'Bend over.'

BEND OVER » 10

RUN! » 17

5

Adrenalin pumps through your body. You grab the alien general's hand, twist and throw him to the ground, judo-style.

'We-are-not-WEAK!' you yell, as you pummel his chest with punches. 'Aaagh!'

Your fist drives through his armour and you withdraw it, finding yourself clutching his still-beating heart. These Krelurians are not as robust as they would like you to think they are!

He looks at you with amazement and a hint of pride, as he drops to his knees and leaks blood out on the floor.

It's over.

YIKES! YOU DID IT!

TRY AGAIN?

'Retreat!' you shout to Sammy over your comms link. You hit reverse and your hoverjet speeds backwards. A voice crackles in your earpiece.

'Cowards!' the Krelurian roars. 'You will both pay in blood!'

Zipping back, you perform the space equivalent of a handbrake turn and zoom away. 'Come in! I'm in trouble!' Sammy yells over the comms link. 'I can't hold on much – ' KABOOM!

You look up in time to see the other hoverjet explode. Sammy's dismembered arm splats onto your windscreen. Now what?

ATTACK! » 18

SURRENDER » 24

7

The Krelurian vapourises the Grey alien in an instant.

'You betrayed us. You will pay!' the Krelurian general growls. He points his vapourising ray at Sammy, who tries to duck for cover. The Krelurian destroys Sammy with a single blast and turns to you. 'You will suffer as a slave of the Krelurian empire!'

'No! Wait!' you begin, but he presses a syringe to your neck and pushes the needle into a vein. Suddenly you are locked in your own body, awake but totally obedient. He binds your hands with rope — and your new life as a slave begins.

 MEH. THEM'S THE BREAKS. TRY AGAIN?

You slam your hand down on the SOS button. Hopefully a passing craft may be able to help. Moments later, you get another comms call. A grey alien with large, black eyes appears on-screen. 'We come in peace,' it says.

'We're under attack. Can you help?' you ask. You hate to ask, but you feel as though you have no choice.

'We can, but for a price,' says the alien. 'We need all the ore that you have mined.'

All the ore? That's worth billions! And your boss back on Earth would go crazy!

What do you do?

AGREE » 22

DECLINE » 1

9

'Grab this,' you say, handing Sammy a laser cannon. 'Fire at will!'

The door flies off its hinges and the Krelurian general bursts through. Impressive blue beams shoot from your weapons, but the alien just smiles.

'Fools! Krelurian armour is the best in the universe! We feed off laser-cannon fire!'

You try to fire again, but you're out of power. You drop the cannon and the general laughs.

He grasps your head in his massive hand and squeezes, cracking your skull as if he was crushing a grape.

 OUCH! DEAD AGAIN!

TRY AGAIN?

Shaking, you turn around as the creature approaches you.

'This will hurt. A lot,' he says with a nasty smile. As he places his scaly hand on your behind, you feel a burst of adrenalin and you turn to face him.

'No chance, snake-face!' you tell him.

You grab the needle and plunge it deep into his brain. The influx of microspores causes him to froth and foam at the mouth. Shaking and shivering, he falls to the ground and lies still.

You give him a kick to be sure, but he's definitely dead.

GAME OVER. YOU WON! TRY AGAIN?

11

The aliens open fire on each other!
PEW PEW! KA-BLAM! KER-BOOSH!

You grab your crewmate Sammy and hit
the emergency teleport button. Seconds
later, you appear on Moon Unit Five,
from where you see your own Moon Unit
explode in a hail of gunfire.

Finally a radio on your side buzzes — it's
your boss back on Earth.

'Get back to Earth immediately. The
President wants to speak with you. You
may have survived, kid, but you've
probably just lost your job and started an
intergalactic war!'

ALIVE = GOOD. WELL
DONE! TRY AGAIN?

12

In the brig, you call the guard over. 'Come closer!' you say. 'I have something for you!'

The gullible guard steps up close to the bars and you reach out quickly. Grabbing his sidearm, you manage to choke him through the bars. You grab his keys and escape.

You make your way to the cargo hold, where you find a thousand tons of missiles and a radio. With the radio, you could send for help, but with the missiles you could sort this out once and for all.

Which do you choose to use?

MISSILES » 2

RADIO » 21

You take the medal and the gun.

As soon as you hold them, you are overcome with a strange feeling. You feel powerful – and really, really angry. A sea of rage washes over you.

The general smiles and you notice your reflection in the porthole.

You are changing – scales grow on your face. Your hands become claws.

Soon the hideous face of a Krelurian stares back at you.

A TRAITOR, BUT ALIVE
TRY AGAIN?

14

'Ready for action?' you shout.

Crewmate Sammy nods and you each board a hoverjet. They're usually used to blast moon rock whilst mining, but their lasers should work as weapons as well.

'Lock and load! Let's go!' yells Sammy over the hoverjet's motors.

Just then, the alien craft is joined by twenty others, as they blip into space through a transdimensional wormhole.

[Gulp.] What now?

Continue the attack or back away?

ATTACK ANYWAY » 18

RETREAT » 6

You bow your head in submission.

'You will be my slave,' says the alien general.

His right arm sprouts tentacles, each with a sharp needle at the end. The needles enter your skin, injecting a serum which gives you a feeling of euphoria.

Drugged and compliant, you will now spend the rest of your life as a Krelurian slave.

FAREWELL, SLAVE

TRY AGAIN?

16

'Aaaargh!' you yell, as you hurl the axe at the Krelurian.

It spins as it flies but the alien, trained for battle, dodges it easily.

He begins to laugh when ... CRASH! The axe smashes through the porthole and the Krelurian is sucked out onto the moon's surface.

He gasps for breath, but there is no one to help. He suffocates instantly. The safety system seals the hole, saving you and your crew.

'I think it's over,' you say.

GOOD JOB!

TRY AGAIN?

17

You summon your courage and dart for the next room, grabbing Sammy and locking the door behind you.

The alien roars through the door's porthole and bangs on the door.

You smile — those doors are made to withstand explosions, so you're not worried about a puny Krelurian.

You think about your options. In the cargo bay you have 200 tonnes of mining explosives and two laser cannons.

Which do you choose?

EXPLOSIVES » 26

CANNON » 9

Still on your hoverjet, you speed toward the fleet of ships, shooting blindly.

POW! PEW!

A few shots hit their targets, but many miss. The Krelurian ships return fire, knocking you off course.

Your hoverjet is badly damaged and you crash. You are grabbed by soldiers, taken aboard their craft and thrown in the brig.

What's your plan?

BREAK OUT » 12

WAIT » 3

19

You swing the axe at the alien. The strike misses his body completely, so you swing again. This time you manage to lop off his arm.

'**Aaaaargh!**' your crewmate Sammy yells in horror. You give yourself a mental high-five for bravery.

Blood spurts from the severed limb, but the alien's reaction is not quite what you were expecting. The Krelurian general just laughs.

You step back and watch, mesmerised, as his arm regrows in front of you.

'Huh. Now what?' you mutter.

THROW AXE » 16

DROP IT » 4

You shake your head. 'Never!' you say, staring defiantly into the Krelurian's hideous face.

'Very well. The alternative is death,' he says.

You nod. 'Better dead than a traitor.'

You salute and face the general as he raises his gun.

The last thing you feel is a sense of pride as the alien pulls the trigger. (OK, it's not quite the last thing you feel.)

 A NOBLE DEFEAT

TRY AGAIN?

21

'SOS!' you blurt into the radio. 'Do you read me?' You wait for ages, then a hiss comes down the line.

'Come in, Moon Unit One, do you read me?' It's a reply – from your home planet's government.

'Yes!' you shout. 'We're under attack! An alien warship has landed!'

'Sit tight, citizen. We'll fix this.' You do as you're told, but your hope begins to fade. Soon it's clear no one is coming.

No one – except for a nuclear warhead big enough to destroy the whole moon. A present from your government.

KABOOM! YOU WIN AND DIE! TRY AGAIN?

You've no option – a planetary invasion could be next. 'Okay,' you say. 'You can have our ore. But hurry!'

The screen shuts off – but the control panel immediately buzzes. You are being boarded. The Krelurian alien teleports onto the bridge, his large body filling the space.

'You are our prisoners!' he roars. Then there's another click of static as a second alien, tall and grey, teleports in.

'And you are ours!' says the Grey, appearing behind him. The two aliens turn their weapons on each other.

TELEPORT OUT » 11

TAKE COVER » 7

23

'Engage comms,' you bark. 'This is Moon Unit One. We want no trouble here.'

The Krelurian commander laughs.

'Very wise. We take that as your surrender. You must now submit to tagging as new assets in our empire,' says the cracked voice of the alien.

'What?' you blurt out.

'You are slaves now,' explains the Krelurian. 'Prepare to be boarded.'

ARM YOURSELF » 25

SEND FOR HELP » 8

24

You return to the moon unit and surrender.

The Krelurian general materialises in front of you.

'Very wise,' he says. 'Your race is weak. Your planet will suffer and we will crush you.'

You may have surrendered, but you still have pride in your planet and your species. You feel yourself flushing red with anger.

The alien places his scaly hand on your shoulder.

FIGHT! » 5

SUBMIT » 15

You break the glass on the emergency fire axe.

'I'm not going to be a slave and I'm not going down without a fight,' you say.

The Krelurian general teleports onto your bridge.

He's a lot bigger than you realised. You weigh up the axe in your hand.

CHOP HIM » 19

DROP IT » 4

26

'Are you sure about this?' asks Sammy. You place the detonators on the crates of explosive as the Krelurian hammers at the door.

'Um ... yeah. I think so,' you say.

The alien smashes through the door. (So much for it being explosion-proof!)

'You will surrender!' he growls.

'Over my dead body ... and yours,' you say.

You hit the button and Moon Unit One explodes, leaving just a crater behind.

GOOD QUIP! BUT R.I.P.

TRY AGAIN?

THANKS FOR PLAYING

There are lots of ways
your story can turn out.

Why not try again and
pick a different path?

HAVE YOU PICKED YOUR PATH
THROUGH THESE?

ABOUT THE AUTHOR

Born at an early age, Dan Metcalf always loved writing and was the kid who would stay in at breaktime at school **ON PURPOSE** to finish the story he was writing.

Dan is now a professional daydreamer and full-time writer, He thinks that many book people are a bit sniffy about games, and says he wrote **PICK YOUR PATH** to teach them a lesson!